# THE DUBLIN FOX

Written and Illustrated by Kelly Ulrich

INSPIREBYTES
OMNI MEDIA

The Dublin Fox

Distributed globally with Expanded Distribution by KDP.

ISBN Paperback: 978-0-9963668-7-8
ISBN E-Book: 978-0-9963668-8-5

Library of Congress Control Number: 2020943297

◫ INSPIREBYTES OMNI MEDIA

Inspirebytes Omni Media LLC
PO Box 988
Wilmette, IL 60091

For more information, please visit www.inspirebytes.com.

I affectionately dedicate this story to my friend, Candace,

who nearly tripped over that little fox, one Christmas in Dublin.

One winter, not too long ago, I rented a small cottage in Ireland, near Dublin. It was a fine cottage made of stone with two chimneys and a red door.

The cottage was near all the stores, and one afternoon, I needed to go grocery shopping.

When I came out of the store with my bag in my arms, I nearly tripped over something small but soft.

I looked down, and dashing out in front of me was a fox! He glanced at me briefly, then ran across the road and was gone!

I walked home with my groceries, and after putting them away, I sat down with a cup of hot milky tea. Staring out the window, I began to think about that little fox.

I wondered how hard life must be for him. There were so many dangers near a city: cars and dogs, and people with traps.

It was also winter, and food would be scarce.

So, later that night, after dinner, I scraped some pork chops into a bowl and placed it on the back porch.

The snow fell through the night.

In the morning, I looked out the window and saw animal tracks everywhere. Did they belong to my fox?

I was curious, so I checked the bowl. It was empty!

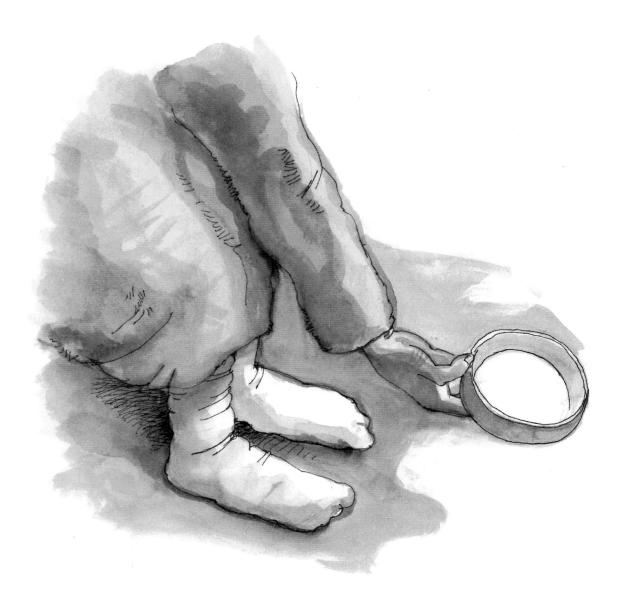

I quickly ate breakfast, gulped the last of my tea, and put on my coat as I hurried out the door to follow the footprints in the snow. They led up the road toward the church.

My little fox was waiting patiently at the side door. I watched from a distance to see what would happen. The door opened, and the priest came out with something in his hand. It was a chicken leg!

"Here you go, my friend. I saved this for you. Enjoy!"

He handed the food to the fox and went back inside.
It took the fox only a few bites before the chicken leg
was gone.

Seeing that the priest seemed to know the fox, I
wondered how many other friends my little fox had
made in the town. So, I decided to follow him throughout the morning.

His next stop was at a fishmongers. There was a little plate by the back entrance with two small fish on it. The fox ate them both in one gulp.

After that we paid a visit to the post office where a cheese sandwich was left outside for him.

And then it was time for dessert! The little fox paid a visit to the local bakery where two cookies were waiting for him.

I followed my furry friend throughout the day, as he stopped to visit all sorts of neighbors.

From breakfast to dinner, they left him stews and soups, and bowls of water or milk. He even ate a plate of spaghetti!

I wondered how long it would be before he could eat no more.

Finally, as the sun was getting low in the sky, my little fox headed toward the trees of a nearby forest. He stopped and looked over his shoulder at me as if to say, "I know you have been following me."

Then, with a flick of his beautiful tail, he disappeared into a low hedge and was gone.

Suddenly, I shivered as a cold wind blew through my coat. I had walked what felt like miles and could use a rest. Not far away I saw a dimly lit sign in the distance. I decided to go in for a warm drink.

As I drew nearer, I looked up at the sign and couldn't believe what I saw. It was called The Dublin Fox!

I hurried in, grateful for the warmth. Sitting down by a window, I asked my waitress "Excuse me, but why is this pub called The Dublin Fox?"

"Why, there have been foxes in Dublin for 800 years or more," she said. Then, giving me a wink, she added: "It's good luck if you see one, you know."

As I sipped my drink, she wiped the table next to mine and continued, "Hundreds of years ago, there were thousands of rats and mice in Dublin. There were too many for the cats. The dogs were fair at catching them, but a local gameskeeper realized there was something more clever than a dog.

A year or two before, he had found an orphaned wild fox kit in the woods. He raised it for company and to keep the rats away from his cottage. So he brought it to town one day, and it did such an amazing job at catching rats, the fox was made the official mascot of Dublin!

From then on, we have always welcomed foxes in our neighborhoods. We share our food with them as a way of saying thank you for ridding us of all the rats."

I smiled as I thought about my day following my little fox friend around the town as he collected his reward for doing his job. I thanked the waitress, paid my bill, and made my way home through the evening snow.

I did not have to worry anymore, as I knew the fox was well taken care of.

Later that night, before turning out the lights and heading to bed, I joined in the tradition and left a little bowl of milk on the back porch.

As I climbed into bed and thought of my little fox and the wonderful story I heard that day, my heart smiled.

Then I fell into a deep happy sleep on a cold winter's night knowing my Dublin Fox would be happy too.

# About the Author/Illustrator
## Kelly Ulrich

Kelly Ulrich, IOM Resident Artist, is a children's book illustrator and author from the west coast of British Columbia, Canada. She attended Emily Carr College of Art and Design and worked in the Graphics Department at the B.C. Teachers' Federation for over 25 years. For the last 15 years she has been involved with teaching art to students of all ages on Vancouver Island and in the Vancouver area.

In addition to illustrating children's books, Kelly recently created the successful comic strip series on Instagram called "Nala, Dean & Vinny." She paints in acrylic, watercolor, and oil.

For more information, visit Kelly on Instagram: @kellyulrichartist.

Manufactured by Amazon.ca
Bolton, ON

15034545R00021